DREAMWORKS

HOW TO TRAIN YOUR
DRAGON
THE HIDDEN WORLD

READY TO FLY!

DREAMWORKS

HOW TO TRAIN YOUR
DRAGON
THE HIDDEN WORLD

READY TO FLY!

studio fun
INTERNATIONAL

THIS...IS BERK!

Welcome to Berk, the world's first dragon-Viking utopia! It's been our home for seven generations with a growing . . . rapidly growing dragon population. We're getting really close to running out of places to house them!

With so many dragons in one location, Berk is a target for evil dragon hunters like Grimmel. When Grimmel paid me an unwelcome surprise visit, unleashing his venomous Deathgrippers upon my house, I needed a plan, and fast. We had to find a new home if we wanted to live in peace with our dragons. Our only option was to disappear off the map, and take the dragons where no hunter or trapper would find them—the Hidden World.

When I was young, my Dad, Stoick, once told me about the Hidden World, a secret land at the edge of the sea where all species of dragons lived peacefully together. We just had to find it!

WELCOME TO NEW BERK...

We set off with as many supplies as two loaded ships and our dragons could carry. The journey was tiresome, with no end in sight. After a good long while, the Hidden World was still hidden to us, and our dragons needed a rest. In fact, we all needed a break, so we decided to temporarily camp on a beautiful island with granite cliffs as high as the clouds and a lush valley with a shimmering lake and crystal cascading waterfalls.

A new dragon—a Light Fury—had followed us to the island. She and Toothless seemed to like each other. Before he hadn't wanted me to fix his tail fin, but now he was interested in flying on his own, so I worked up a new design and now he's able to fly without me. One day, Toothless and the Light Fury flew off together.

They were gone a long time with no sign of where they'd gone to, so Stormfly helped Astrid and me track them down. She led us to a gigantic hole in the sea with enormous flowing waterfalls—it was the entrance to the Hidden World! Inside, it was an otherworldly sight with fluorescent coral-speckled structures. Hundreds and hundreds of dragons were flying, resting, playing—they were all living here! Their scales also glowed in the vast underground cavern. It was unlike anything we had ever seen.

AND THE HIDDEN WORLD!

After realizing the mysterious Hidden World was meant only for dragons, we headed back to our temporary camp. All the Vikings had started to feel at home there, so we decided to make it official. In honor of our previous residence that we'd built over seven generations, we've named our current glorious island home New Berk.

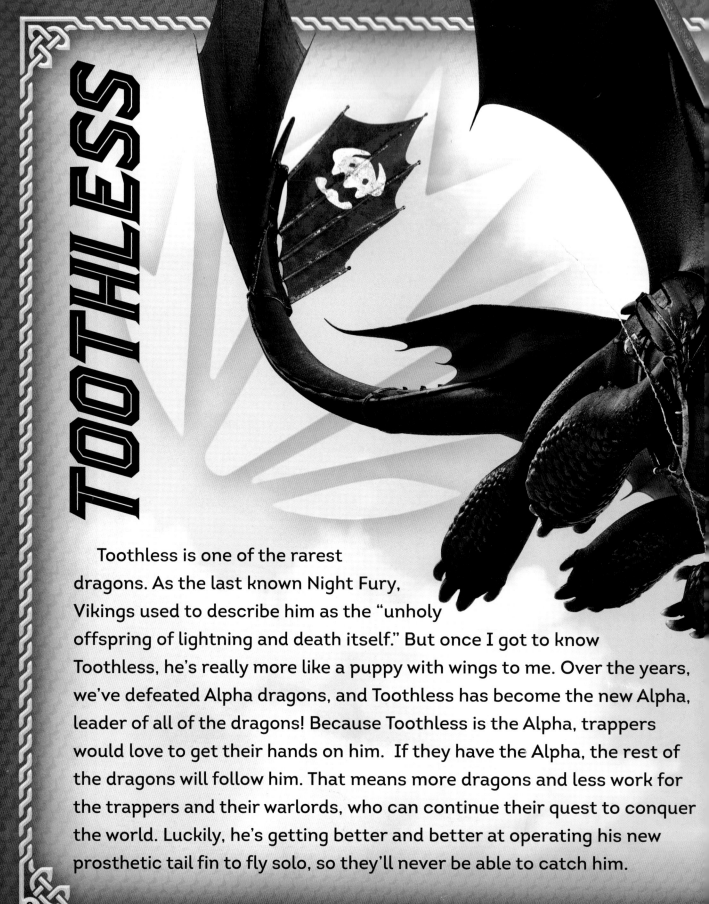

TOOTHLESS

Toothless is one of the rarest dragons. As the last known Night Fury, Vikings used to describe him as the "unholy offspring of lightning and death itself." But once I got to know Toothless, he's really more like a puppy with wings to me. Over the years, we've defeated Alpha dragons, and Toothless has become the new Alpha, leader of all of the dragons! Because Toothless is the Alpha, trappers would love to get their hands on him. If they have the Alpha, the rest of the dragons will follow him. That means more dragons and less work for the trappers and their warlords, who can continue their quest to conquer the world. Luckily, he's getting better and better at operating his new prosthetic tail fin to fly solo, so they'll never be able to catch him.

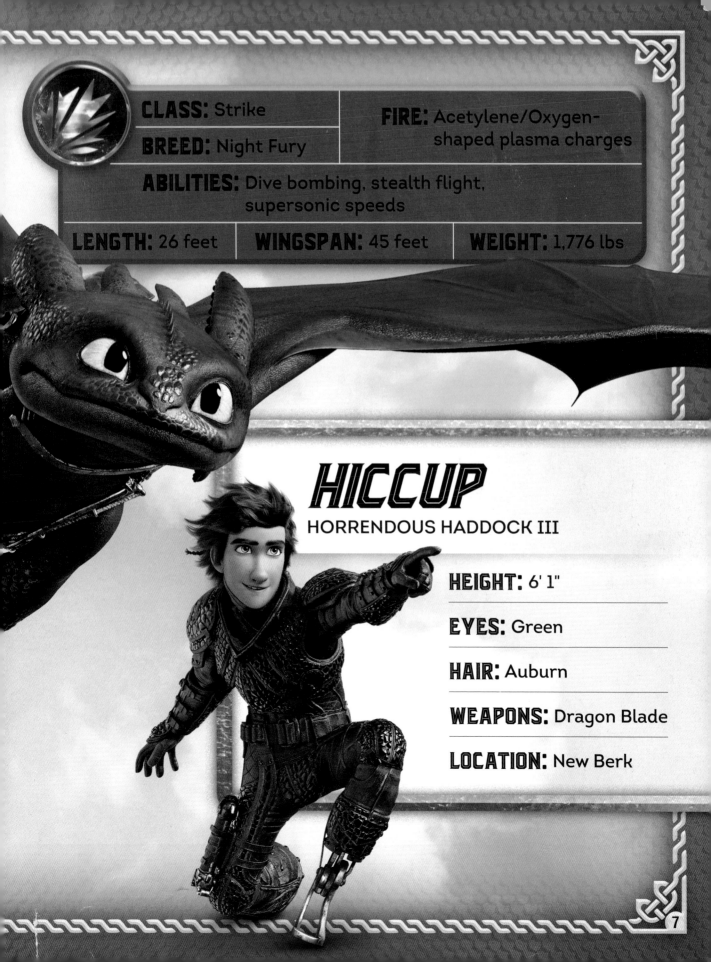

CLASS: Strike

BREED: Night Fury

FIRE: Acetylene/Oxygen-shaped plasma charges

ABILITIES: Dive bombing, stealth flight, supersonic speeds

LENGTH: 26 feet

WINGSPAN: 45 feet

WEIGHT: 1,776 lbs

HICCUP

HORRENDOUS HADDOCK III

HEIGHT: 6' 1"

EYES: Green

HAIR: Auburn

WEAPONS: Dragon Blade

LOCATION: New Berk

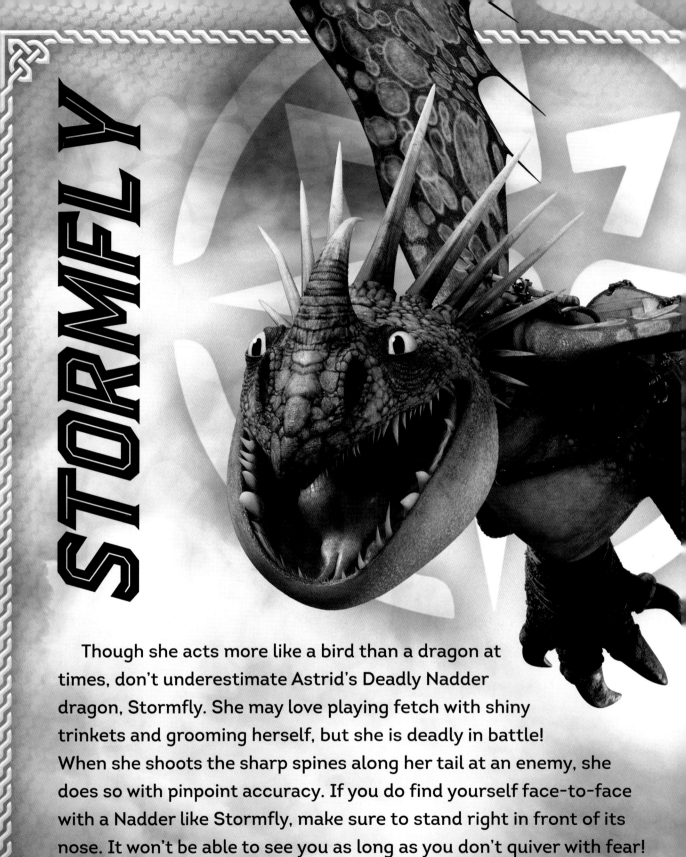

STORMFLY

Though she acts more like a bird than a dragon at times, don't underestimate Astrid's Deadly Nadder dragon, Stormfly. She may love playing fetch with shiny trinkets and grooming herself, but she is deadly in battle! When she shoots the sharp spines along her tail at an enemy, she does so with pinpoint accuracy. If you do find yourself face-to-face with a Nadder like Stormfly, make sure to stand right in front of its nose. It won't be able to see you as long as you don't quiver with fear!

CLASS: Tracker

BREED: Deadly Nadder

FIRE: Magnesium

ABILITIES: Spine shots with deadly accuracy

LENGTH: 30 feet **WINGSPAN:** 42 feet **WEIGHT:** 2,628 lbs

ASTRID
HOFFERSON

HEIGHT: 5' 9"

EYES: Blue

HAIR: Blonde

WEAPONS: Axe

LOCATION: New Berk

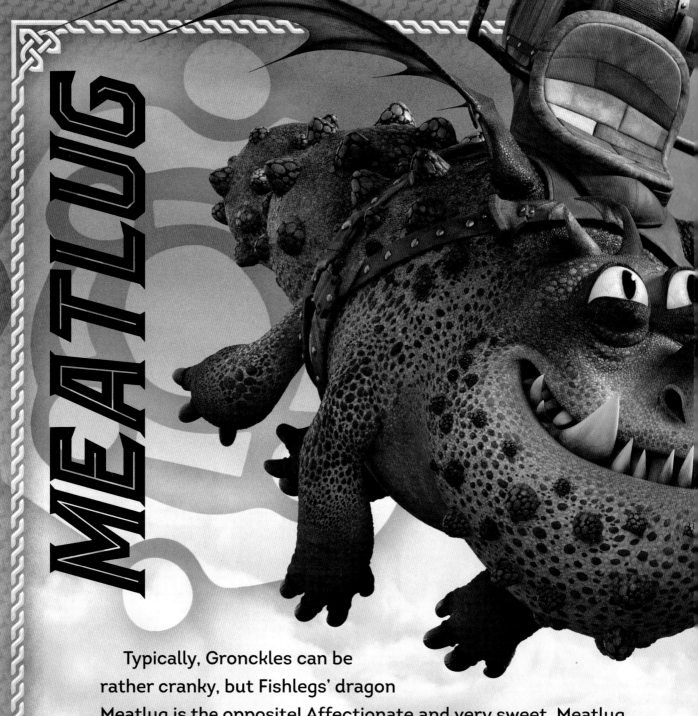

MEATLUG

Typically, Gronckles can be
rather cranky, but Fishlegs' dragon
Meatlug is the opposite! Affectionate and very sweet, Meatlug
does everything with her rider, Fishlegs, whether they're flying
through the clouds or fighting together in battle. The massive
Gronckles are the only dragons that can fly backwards or side
to side like a helicopter. If you see a Gronckle eating rocks, look
out! It may be about to spew a scorching lava blast!

CLASS: Boulder	**FIRE:** Heptane/Oxygen +
BREED: Gronckle	rock = lava attack

ABILITIES: Shoots flaming chunks of rock and lava

LENGTH: 14 feet	**WINGSPAN:** 18 feet	**WEIGHT:** 5,724 lbs

FISHLEGS

INGERMAN

HEIGHT: 5' 9"

EYES: Green

HAIR: Blonde

WEAPONS: Dragon Knowledge

LOCATION: New Berk

FISHMEAT

Fishmeat, like all Gronckles, has a very round body and tiny wings. Yet, although they are small, they have incredible flapping velocity. As a young dragon, Fishmeat needs lots of naps and has occasionally been known to fall asleep mid-flight. Whether he's teething, eating stones, or taking naps, Fishmeat is lucky to have Fishlegs caring for him and carrying him around everywhere.

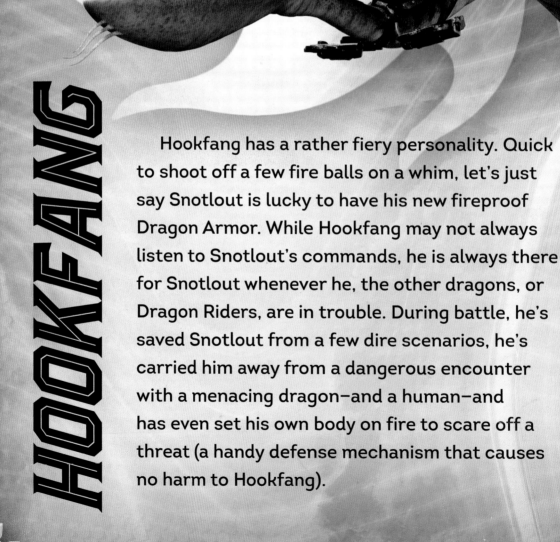

HOOKFANG

Hookfang has a rather fiery personality. Quick to shoot off a few fire balls on a whim, let's just say Snotlout is lucky to have his new fireproof Dragon Armor. While Hookfang may not always listen to Snotlout's commands, he is always there for Snotlout whenever he, the other dragons, or Dragon Riders, are in trouble. During battle, he's saved Snotlout from a few dire scenarios, he's carried him away from a dangerous encounter with a menacing dragon—and a human—and has even set his own body on fire to scare off a threat (a handy defense mechanism that causes no harm to Hookfang).

CLASS: Stoker

BREED: Monstrous Nightmare

FIRE: Kerosene

ABILITIES: When threatened, Monstrous Nightmares emit kerosene gel through their pores and then breathe fire, which sets their bodies aflame

LENGTH: 61 feet

WINGSPAN: 68 feet

WEIGHT: 5,040 lbs

SNOTLOUT

JORGENSON

HEIGHT: 5' 3"

EYES: Blue

HAIR: Brown

WEAPONS: Hammer

LOCATION: New Berk

BARF & BELCH

Barf and Belch are Ruffnut and Tuffnut's double-headed dragon. They say two heads are better than one, and that's definitely true for this duo. While Barf breathes flammable green gas, Belch sparks it creating a one-two punch that creates a massive explosion. Even without Belch's flame, Barf's gas is enough to provide adequate cover for evading capture or attack. If they're looking to cause some extra destruction, they create fire, bite their own tails, and spin, making themselves look like a wheel of flames to knock out their opponents like bowling pins!

CLASS: Mystery

BREED: Hideous Zippleback

FIRE: Ammonium Nitrate mixes with Anhydrous Hydrazine

ABILITIES: BARF: Emits flammable gas
BELCH: Creates a spark that ignites the gas
BOTH: Transform into flaming wheel-of-death

LENGTH: 66 feet **WINGSPAN:** 38 feet **WEIGHT:** 6,036 lbs

TUFFNUT & RUFFNUT

THORSTON

HEIGHT: 5' 9"

EYES: Blue

HAIR: Blonde

WEAPONS: Mace and Spear

LOCATION: New Berk

LIGHT FURY

CLASS: Strike

BREED: Light Fury

FIRE: Acetylene/Oxygen-shaped plasma charges

ABILITIES: Camouflage, stealth flight

LENGTH: 22 feet

WINGSPAN: 42 feet

WEIGHT: 1,600 lbs

Another very rare dragon, the Light Fury, is a type of dragon we didn't even know existed! When she first met Toothless, she was pretty skittish about us humans, but once she got to know us—after she fired off a few plasma blasts at us—she was more comfortable. As fast as Toothless, the Light Fury can also blend into the sky no matter what time of day thanks to her mirror-like scales that reflect her surroundings. When she blasts a fireball and flies through it, she disappears into thin air. Though she would rather fly without a rider, the Light Fury will tolerate one to defend a good cause.

Berk is more than a place. Our people are what make Berk so special. No matter how many miles of endless sea we travel, we will always have our traditions and each other. And though some traditions may need to be tweaked, that just makes us even stronger whether we're exploring new horizons, discovering new dragons like the Light Fury, or searching for a new place to lay our heads. Hopefully, one day, all humans and dragons can live in peace, and trappers and hunters will be things of the past. Until then, us loyal Berkians will stick together, continuing to protect dragons and creating new traditions for future generations.

DRAGON ASSEMBLY

ASSEMBLY TIP

Although regular transparent tape is okay to use, we recommend double-sided transparent tape to make the best-looking dragons.

FLIGHT TIPS

- Make sure all parts are taped firmly in place.
- Double-check the tape on the dragon's head. Don't leave any openings to catch air.
- Check for symmetry—make sure the left side looks the same as the right side.
- Most dragons fly best with a good, hard throw. Grip the body near the legs and throw it slightly upward.
- The wings and tail should be either flat or bent slightly upward for best flight.

STORMFLY

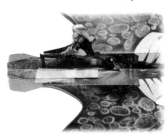

1. Find and fold all the pieces.

2. Turn the dragon over. Position the neck piece by lining up the art, and tape.

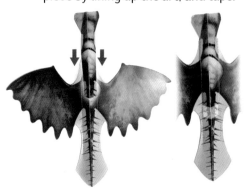

3. Add Astrid as shown and tape.

4. Squeeze the head together, and tape down the tab on the inside.

5. Slide the head over the horn. Then tape the head to the neck.

6. Position the legs by lining up the art, and tape them in place.

HOOKFANG

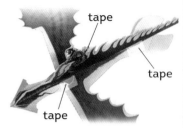

1. Find and fold all the pieces.

2. Fold back the wing supports, and tape.

3. Tape down Snotlout on the three tabs.

tape

tape

tape

4. Add the head piece by squeezing the neck slightly and taping down.

5. Position the legs by lining up the art, and tape them in place.

6. Make sure Snotlout is standing straight.

BARF & BELCH

1. Find and fold all the pieces.

2. Fold the wings together, and tape.

3. Add the head and neck piece to the top of the body, and tape.

4. Add the legs to the body by lining up the art, and tape.

5. Fold the small tabs on Ruffnut and Tuffnut and insert them through the slots on the neck piece.

6. Tape the supports down as shown.

tape

MEATLUG

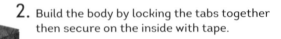

1. Find and fold all the pieces.

2. Build the body by locking the tabs together then secure on the inside with tape.

tape

5. Attach the head by folding the small tabs and inserting them into the slots on the body. Then attach Fishlegs.

3. Fold in the small tabs and insert it through the slit on the head. Unfold the tabs to lock it together.

4. Insert tabs on the wings into the slots on the body.

FISHMEAT

1. Find and fold all the pieces.

2. Build the body by locking the tabs together then secure on the inside with tape.

5. Attach the head by folding the small tabs and inserting them into the slots on the body.

3. Fold in the small tabs and insert it through the slit on the head. Unfold the tabs to lock it together.

4. Insert tabs on the wings into the slots on the body.

TOOTHLESS & LIGHT FURY

1. Find and fold all the pieces for Toothless. *

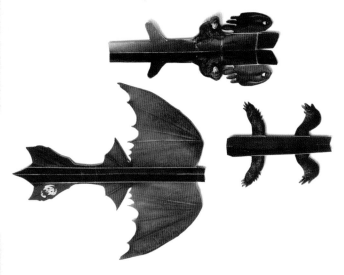

2. Fold the head weights back, and tape to secure.

3. Place the legs over the head piece. Then slide the belly through the slit.

4. Tape the leg piece to the head piece.

5. Now add the head and legs to the wing piece. Line up with the gray box as shown, and secure with tape.

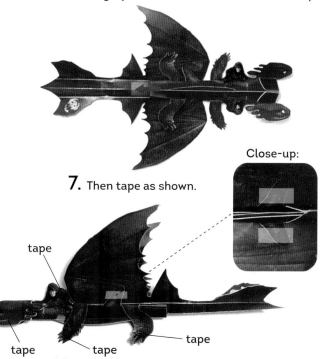

6. Fold both sides of the dragon's head down, and fold the dragon in the center. Next, fold down the legs so they touch.

7. Then tape as shown.

Close-up:

tape

tape

tape

tape

* Repeat instructions for Light Fury. (rider not included)

TOOTHLESS

LIGHT FURY

HOOKFANG

STORMFLY

BARF & BELCH

MEATLUG

FISHMEAT